SEEING STARS

written and illustrated by Sharleen Collicott

DIAL BOOKS FOR YOUNG READERS *New York*

Published by Dial Books for Young Readers
A Division of Penguin Books USA Inc.
375 Hudson Street
New York, New York 10014

Copyright © 1996 by Sharleen Collicott
All rights reserved
Design by Nancy R. Leo
Printed in Hong Kong
First Edition
1 3 5 7 9 10 8 6 4 2

Library of Congress Cataloging in Publication Data
Collicott, Sharleen.
Seeing stars / written and illustrated by Sharleen Collicott. — 1st ed.
p.   cm.
Summary: Junkyard animals Motley and Fuzzball build a
junkbird and fly to what they think are the stars.
ISBN 0-8037-1522-6 — ISBN 0-8037-1523-4
[1. Animals—Fiction. 2. Flight—Fiction.] I. Title.
PZ7.C67758Se 1996   [E]—dc20   93-49846   CIP   AC

The art was rendered in gouache.
It was then color-separated and reproduced in full color.

Thank you, Eric William Pederson

Lots of small animals made their homes in the junkyard.
Motley and Fuzzball lived in a broken teapot, near the old tires.
One evening Motley complained, "I'm tired of this place."

"I want to travel and see new things…like those stars up there."
"STARS!" gasped Fuzzball. "You know we can't fly."
"The birds don't have any trouble flying to the stars," Motley said.
"It can't be that difficult."

The next day Motley was up early. "We can use some of this junk
to build our own bird…a junkbird!" he said.
"Birds fly much too high for me," sighed Fuzzball. "I can help
you build the junkbird, but I don't want to fly in it."

Fuzzball sealed the cracks with tar.
Motley tightened all the screws.
Fuzzball painted on eyes.
Motley added feathers and said, "Isn't this bird beautiful!"

"Fuzzball, I'm *sure* our junkbird will get us to the stars."
"Well, I'm *not* so sure," worried Fuzzball. "If I go with you,
 will we come right back?"
"Of course we will."

"Ready, Fuzzball? STARS, HERE WE COME!"
The junkbird flew in circles.

Motley and Fuzzball shut their eyes tight.
They were bounced around so much, they never heard the splash.

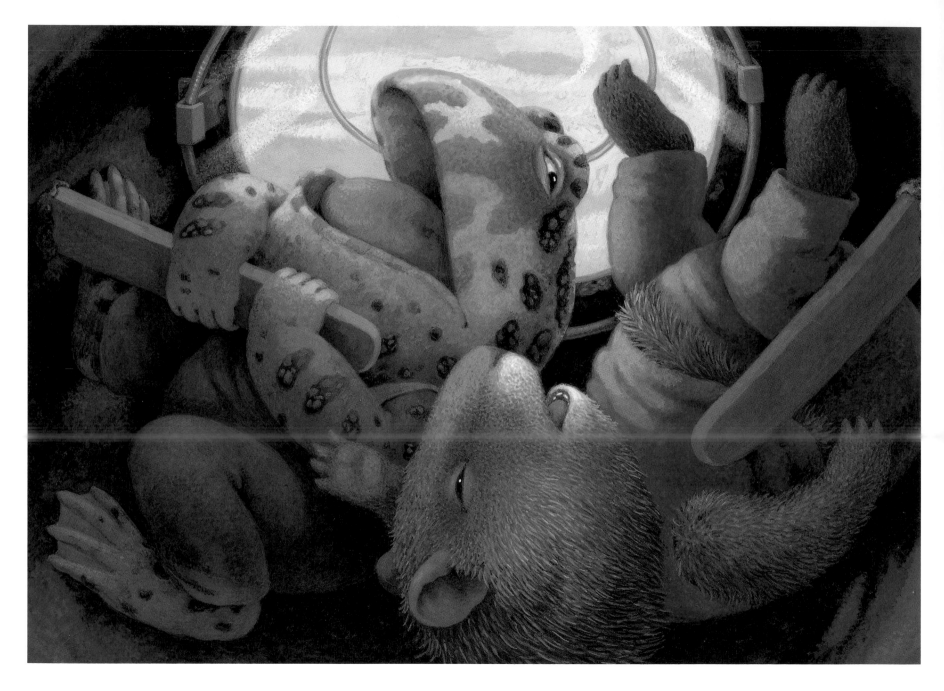

Motley shouted, "Hold on to your wing-stick!
Help me fly this bird straight."

Finally they looked out the junkbird's window.
"We're on our way!" Motley said. "Hey, look at all those strange trees."

"Stars ahead!" he shouted.

"These stars are vicious!" Fuzzball cried. "Watch out for our tail."
They flew away as fast as they could.

"Motley, I think we should go home right now."
Motley wasn't listening.

"MORE STARS," he cheered. "Let's go get a closer look."
"We're already too close," Fuzzball moaned. "They're crawling all over us!"

The crawly stars had never seen anything like the junkbird before.
"What is this thing?" the stars asked each other. "We better drag it to
the fish. They're smart. They will know what to do with it."

"Help! Help! We're being kidnapped!" Fuzzball cried.
"Oh no, we're not," Motley growled. "I'm getting this junkbird away from here."
But the crawly stars hung on tightly.

"Let go of our junkbird, or I'll come out there," Motley threatened.
"Get down, Motley. I don't like the looks of those stars."
    Motley crouched down. "Hey! Where is this water coming from?"

The crawly stars began to move the junkbird downward.
"I'm dizzy," Fuzzball whispered. "I need fresh air. But don't
open the door, whatever you do."

Motley peeked out.
The biggest fish said to the crawly stars, "This thing has some feathers.
It must be a bird…"

"and if it's a bird, it needs air!"
The biggest fish grabbed the junkbird and swam to the surface.

He sailed the junkbird up into the air.
"From now on, be careful where you fly," yelled the fish.
Fuzzball spotted old tires in the distance.
"We're almost home!"

"I told you I could get us back safely," declared Motley.
"Yes, but you didn't tell me that the stars would be so scary."

THUMP! C-R-R-R-UNCH!

The junkyard animals came running.
"Where have you been? What's that broken thing you're in?"
"We've been up in the sky with the stars," Motley bragged.

"Will you take me to the stars?" asked a garbage gopher.
"I want to see the stars too." "Me too! Me too!" all the others shouted.
"Fuzzball, get up. Let's take them to the stars!" said Motley.

"Fine. But this time we'll build junk*stars* so we can see them right here,"
said Fuzzball.
And that's what they did.

Fuzzball never flew again, and he couldn't have been happier.
Motley was too busy to notice....He was working on building a junk*fish*
so they could travel to the deep, deep sea!